BIGFOOT™ FUN BOOK!

PUZZLES, COLORING PAGES, FUN FACTS!

D. L. MILLER

Happy Fox
BOOKS

Dedicated to kids of all ages, parents and grandparents, teachers and librarians who see every day as a new adventure to explore and learn about this great big world we live in!

© 2018 by D. L. Miller and Happy Fox Books, an imprint of Fox Chapel Publishing Company, Inc., 903 Square Street, Mount Joy, PA 17552.

BigFoot Fun Book! is an original work, first published in 2018 by Fox Chapel Publishing Company, Inc.

ISBN 978-1-64124-018-5

To learn more about the other great books from Fox Chapel Publishing, or to find a retailer near you, call toll-free 800-457-9112 or visit us at *www.FoxChapelPublishing.com*.

We are always looking for talented authors. To submit an idea, please send a brief inquiry to acquisitions@foxchapelpublishing.com.

Fox Chapel Publishing makes every effort to use environmentally friendly paper for printing.

Printed in China
First printing

The myth of BigFoot has never been told,
although his legend is very, very old.

He's been among us for many a year,
discovering the world, going far and near.

Few have seen his awesome stride,
but have no doubt, he's been by our side.

He was born in the deep forest amid the shady trees,
sharing his days with the animals and the honeybees.

As he grew older, he started to believe
that the world was full of magic and people he must see.

Leaving his wooded hideaway, he had made up his mind
to eagerly cross this great world one giant step at a time.

With every new day BigFoot was on his way,
making new friends and learning as he played.

Although sightings of this friendly giant are very rare indeed,
he's always out there with us, if we just believe.

This life is an adventure best traveled with friends,
discovering the world together and exploring around each bend.

Along with BigFoot, we all must agree
that this world is a magical place for you and me.

Beaches are made up of loose rock,
sand, gravel, pebbles, and shells.

Can you find **12 things** different on this page?

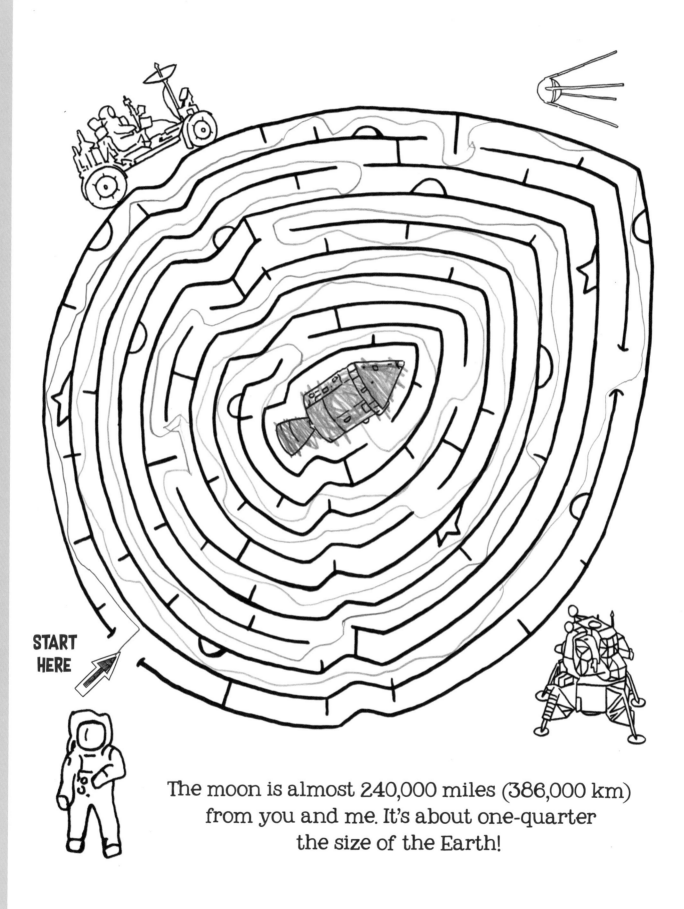

START HERE

The moon is almost 240,000 miles (386,000 km) from you and me. It's about one-quarter the size of the Earth!

Across

2 Always flowing

5 House in the woods

9 Can be climbed

10 Has a lot of teeth and swims

Down

1 Wears a mane and roars

3 Goes to the moon

4 Rarely spotted

6 King's home

7 Has petals

8 Most can see from high above

See page 126 for the answers.

Can you solve these riddles?

Hint: All of the answers have the letter *B*.

1. **What is not a bee but loves honey?** B _ _ _ _ _

2. **What keeps you warm but is not a fire?** B _ _ _ _ _ _ _

3. **I'm bright yellow and always stopping.**
   _ _ _ _ _ _ _ B _ _ _

4. **Before breakfast time, it's...** B _ _ _ _ _ _ _ _ _

5. **Before I can walk, I crawl.** B _ _ b _ _

6. **Rain bounces off my top.** _ _ _ b _ _ _ _ _ _

7. **I wear stripes day or night.** _ _ _ b _ _ _

8. **What travels in herds but rarely is heard.** B _ _ _ _ _ _ _ _

9. **Most people know me for my stripes and how much I like flowers.** B _ _ _ b _ _ _ b _ _ _

10. **I'm full of air and often found during vacations near the water.**
    B _ _ _ _ _ _ B _ _ _ _

See page 126 for the answers.

The biggest hot-air balloon festival in the world is held every year in Albuquerque, New Mexico, with over 500 balloons!

Can you find 10 things different on this page?

BigFoot's Famous Word Scramble

Hint: All the words on the list are types of **Birds.**

1. lgeae   _ _ _ _ _ _

2. driaclan   _ _ _ _ _ _ _ _

3. orwc   _ _ _ _

4. poenig   _ _ _ _ _ _

5. brino   _ _ _ _ _

6. ahkw   _ _ _ _

7. tisohcr   _ _ _ _ _ _ _

8. ubzrazd   _ _ _ _ _ _ _

9. edvo   _ _ _ _

10. uelbrdib   _ _ _ _ _ _ _ _

See page 126 for the answers.

Can you find 10 cats in the herd of cows?

START HERE

There are over 340 different types of hummingbirds in the world. The smallest is called the bee hummingbird and is less than 2 inches (5 cm) long.

Oceans & Seas

```
X Q F O F I T H M T T C F T W Z B
H V I G D S I Z S W V F H V W N E
B H I S L E H T X F C W J G D Y D
A S T N M O R P E J I G D I R R G
L W A C U N N B K W T Q I Z C P K
T F J I O F S I K L C O L P I I F
I C S T O A B W S C R S A I F X L
C L X N G V H A T H A D E N I P R
Y D A A I Y E L L O W Y Z K C E J
E P I L P J O I K Z P Z N V A N O
M A C T W P P Z B U S B O K P N V
K N P A C M V K G E P R S W O A I
C A R I B B E A N Z R M I G B F O
S I T C G X K M B Z E I C Z G A M
J D C O R A L G Y S W U N B W N F
P N N K C H T R O N T I K G D M B
W I N A E N A R R E T I D E M N S
```

Bering	Mediterranean	Caribbean	Atlantic
Yellow	Indian	Red	Arctic
North	Coral	Baltic	Pacific

See page 128 for the answers.

Let's finish drawing the bear!

Did you know a bear can run faster than a human, and smell 100 times better than a human's nose?

Can you solve these riddles?

Hint: All of the answers have the letter *E*.

1. **What has 4 legs and a flat top?** __ e __ __ __

2. **I can be either red, green, or yellow.** __ __ __ __ __ e

3. **Flowers love me!** __ e e

4. **I move by sliding along the ground.** __ __ __ __ __ e

5. **Where do you find a bunch of corn all in a row?** E __ __ __

6. **I always carry a trunk.** E __ __ e __ __ __ __ __ __

7. **What can only be entered with a door?** __ __ __ __ __ e

8. **I'm a flower, but be careful when touching my stem!** __ __ __ __ e

9. **When you visit me, you may find flowers or vegetables, or both!** __ __ __ __ __ __ e __

10. **A day when pumpkins have faces.** __ __ __ __ __ __ __ e e __

See page 126 for the answers.

Across

3 Opens when it rains
4 Keeps the doctor away
6 Loves bananas
8 Always under our foot
9 Sweet treat

Down

1 Carries a lot of children
2 Carries a great trunk
5 Wears a big nose and shoes
6 Paper or coins
7 Black bird

See page 126 for the answers.

Can you find **10 parrots** in the palm trees?

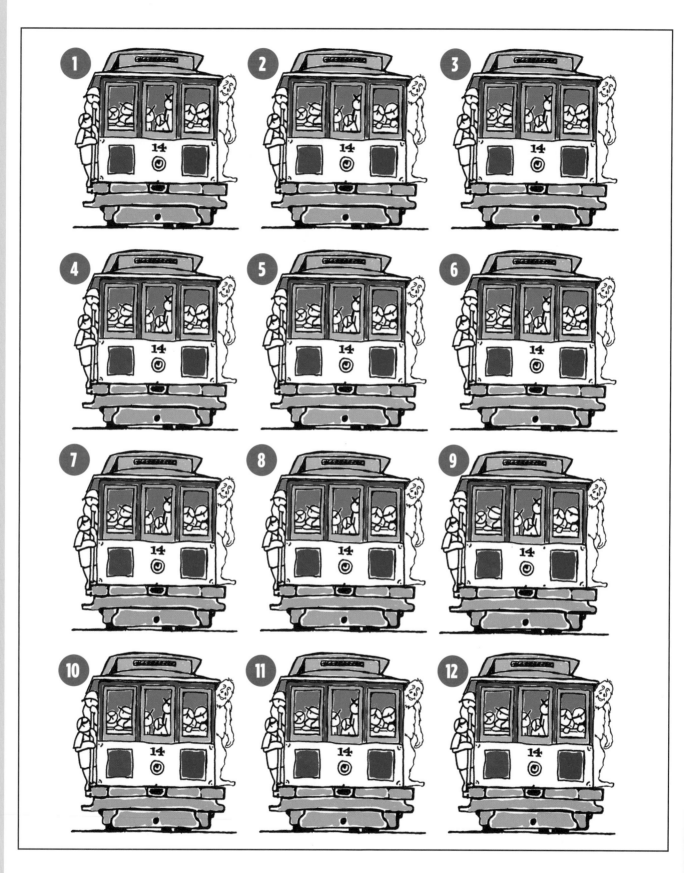

Which trolley car is different?

See page 126 for the answer.

Can you solve these riddles?

Hint: All of the answers have the letter *l.*

1. **What can you climb but is not a tree?** __ __ __ __ __ __ __ __ i __

2. **What can only be reached by boat?** l __ __ __ __ __ __

3. **What holds your hand?** __ __ i __ __

4. **What has 4 legs and rhymes with blizzard?** __ i __ __ __ __

5. **What can you see through when it is closed or open?** __ i __ __ __ __

6. **What is black and goes around?** __ i __ __

7. **What can see from a tree?** __ i __ __ __

8. **What has many cars and follows tracks ?** __ __ __ __ i __

9. **Moves with fins?** __ i __ __

10. **A spotted animal who can see above all others.** __ i __ __ __ __ __

See page 126 for the answers.

Birds

```
B J T Q O G T Q V T L B O C K I L
B S C O O B U Q U W O S H A N G Q
U I W M O A L P O X P R O M U K V
A N S F I P W B E O Y S R U I Q X
W U I L D V B S F L T M W A G Q O
S E E H Y S R W Y R I R U C P O Z
Y U T X K G S F I Q R C A A I X S
C L U E V R F C H D L Y A Y Y C R
R M R S B W H I G L L D C N J H C
A U K R N L T H N E U G U O N D Q
N S E F H U M M I N G B I R D O T
E S Y Q M J J E N H A G G T Z O Y
W Q O N Y U V O P G E K L Q Q F C
C I Z W Y L E G R A S A V X C C D
Z K M X H G W F L A M I N G O F R
P U G D I S U Z H J K Y D D T I V
Y K M P S L D R A Z Z U B B A U K
```

Pelican	Quail	Parrot	Buzzard
Pigeon	Turkey	Hummingbird	Seagull
Crane	Ostrich	Flamingo	Owl

See page 128 for the answers.

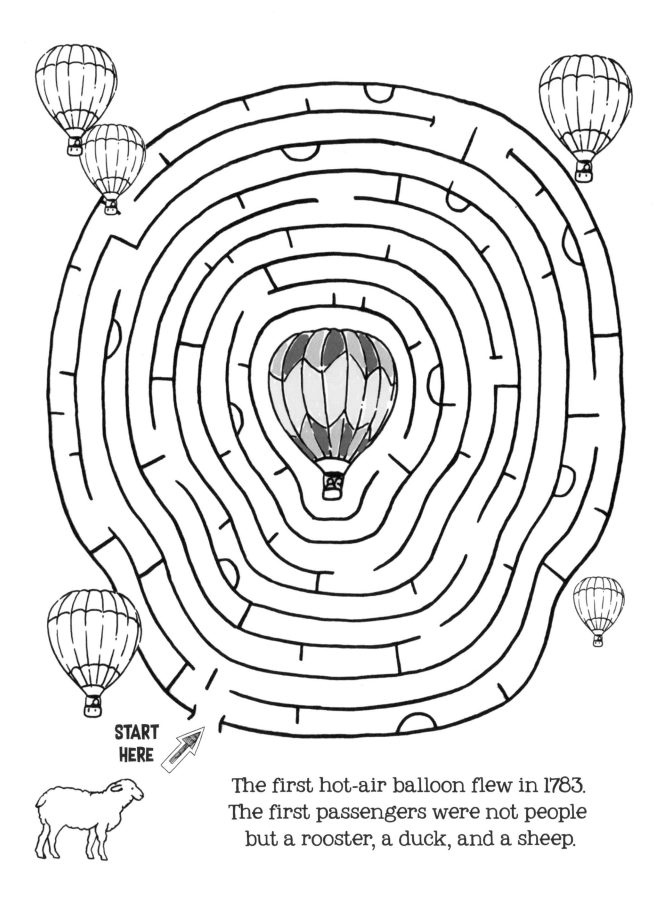

START HERE

The first hot-air balloon flew in 1783. The first passengers were not people but a rooster, a duck, and a sheep.

Which dragon
is different?

See page 126 for the answer.

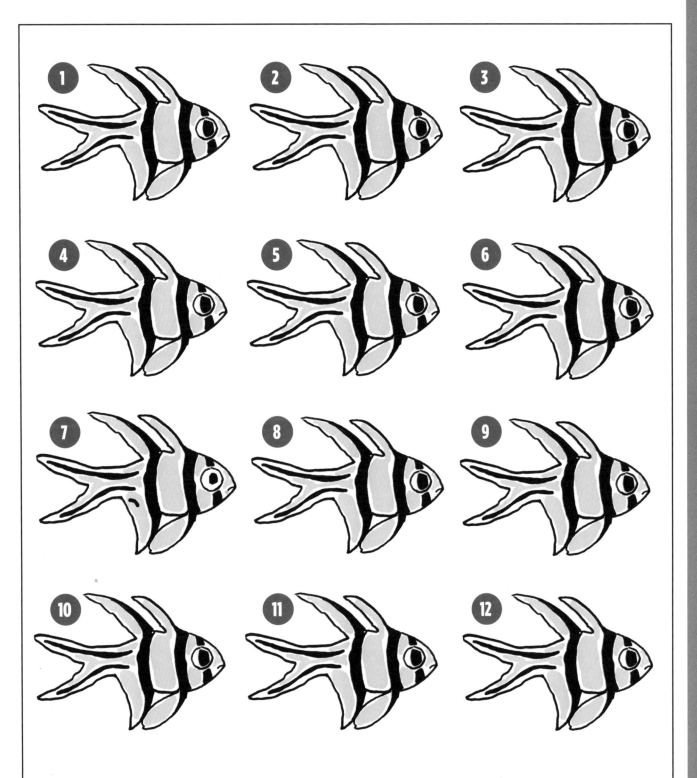

Which cardinal fish is different?

See page 126 for the answer.

Can you find **10 sheep** with the sheepdogs?

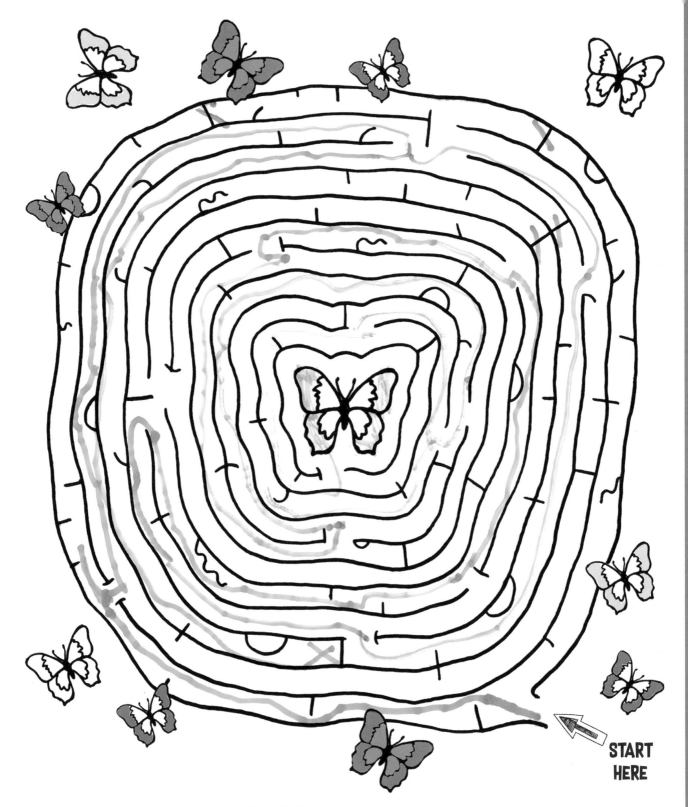

START HERE

Butterflies don't have mouths. Instead, they
have a long, straw-like body part that they use
to drink nectar or other liquids.

Can you finish drawing our friendly Martian from Mars?

In case you ever decide to travel to Mars, pack a lunch. Mars is nearly 34 million miles (55 million km) from Earth!

Across

3 8 legs

4 Need 60 of them to pass time

5 Headlines found at the top

7 Can cross a river

8 Eats oats

9 A place to see art

Down

1 Can be found in Egypt

2 Fly in a V

6 Twisted snack

7 Sandwiches need this

See page 126 for the answers.

Draw... Write... Imagine!

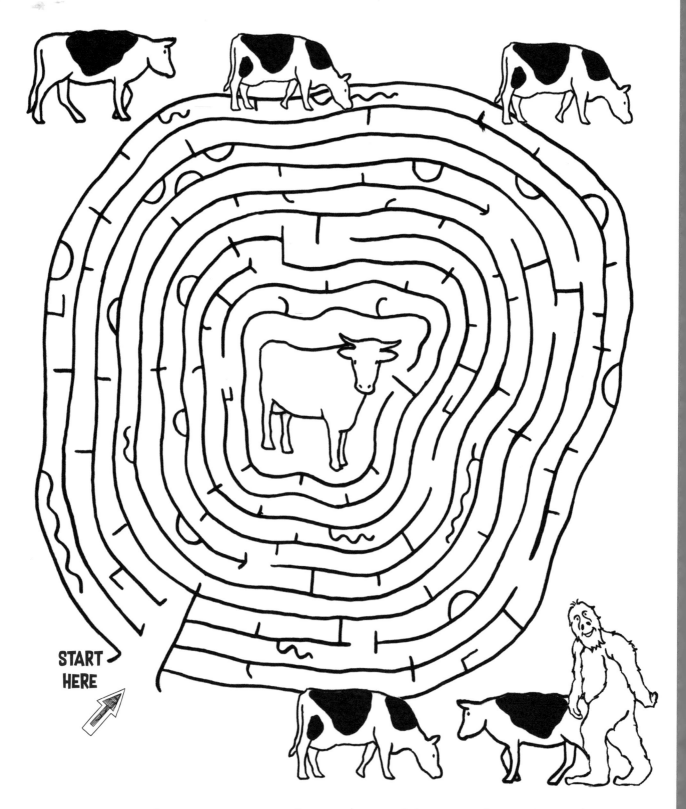

START HERE

An average dairy cow weighs over 1,200 pounds (544 kg) and will drink up to 50 gallons (4 l) of water every day.

Can you solve these riddles?

Hint: All of the answers have the letter *M*.

1. **You can see it when you look up, after the sun goes down.**
   M _ _ _ _

2. **What can be climbed but has no leaves?**
   M _ _ _ _ _ _ _ _

3. **What are you doing when a fire and a tent are needed?**
   _ _ _ m _ _ _ _ _

4. **Some people like me with ketchup, some do not!**
   _ _ _ m _ _ _ _ _ _ _

5. **What gives directions but cannot speak?** M _ _ _

6. **Alligators call me home.** _ _ _ _ m _

7. **I love cheese and tiny places.** M _ _ _ _ _ _

8. **Cookies like me.** M _ _ _ _

9. **A great place for a tractor.** _ _ _ _ m _

10. **What is used to find places?**
    _ _ _ m _ _ _ _ _

See page 126 for the answers.

43

The first Ferris wheel was invented by
George W. Ferris in 1893.

Can you find 11 things different on this page?

Trees

```
V N D K X S M I J F O F F G M A I
M K P N V E V I L O B H X J H O L
Z T R B Q U V R J M I X X S U B I
G R L O U G X Z L F N P W T U W I
X T M E Q U S P R U C E K E F R Z
Y S Q O U A W T I C T U L D S R C
A B U Y J P D H Z E G M V G E P E
D Q E A L P C E N D K A S C J G R
L J B M L L M U H O E A S X F C O
D S M O O E H W A G L G O H N L M
B D B D E J R I V W J Y G H Y K A
L M W G A A J Q M O H T W C P S C
A A X P F H E A D O K K F Y P Q Y
S P H R E A G X O D Y N C E N R S
L L S T N R M B E H X O N E K X N
U E G L I A X A T C B L E H V O I
H W O G P Y U K O T S U C O L J U
```

Pine	Olive	Oak	Elm
Sycamore	Maple	Dogwood	Ash
Locust	Spruce	Aspen	Apple

See page 128 for the answers.

Can you find the 10 clown fish in the crowd of clowns?

Let's finish drawing the school bus!

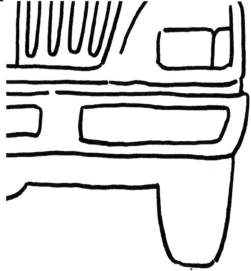

Did you know the official color
for school buses has been yellow
since 1939?

48

Across

1 In charge of the ship

3 Works with a mouse

5 Goes with fries

6 Where rain comes from

8 Sometimes comes in a bar

9 Fruit that grows on a tree

Down

1 King me

2 Travels under the sea

4 Fast cat

7 Takes care of people

See page 126 for the answers.

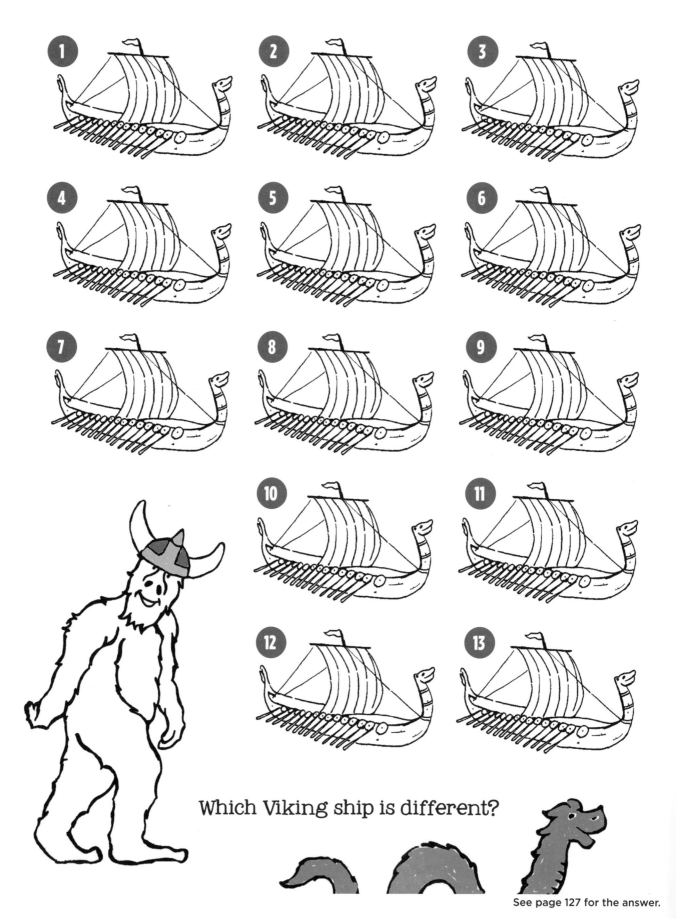

Which Viking ship is different?

See page 127 for the answer.

50

BigFoot's Famous Word Scramble

Hint: All the words on the list are types of **Sports and Games.**

1. olafobtl _ _ _ _ _ _ _ _

2. skecrehc _ _ _ _ _ _ _ _

3. isgnki _ _ _ _ _ _

4. gbnio _ _ _ _ _

5. lbslbaea _ _ _ _ _ _ _ _

6. shesc _ _ _ _ _

7. ict cta eto _ _ _ _ _ _ _ _ _

8. nsient _ _ _ _ _ _

9. ychkoe _ _ _ _ _ _

10. corsce _ _ _ _ _ _

See page 127 for the answers.

Can you solve these riddles?

Hint: All of the answers have the letter O.

1. **I'm rarely spotted but always leave a footprint.**
   __ __ __ __ __ O O __

2. **What sound can you hear at night in the woods?** __ O O __

3. **I have 8 arms and 9 brains!** O __ __ __ O __ __ __ __

4. **When I'm not closed, I'm...** O __ __ __ __

5. **I cover over 70% of our world!** O __ __ __ __ __

6. **Who lives in the north but is hard to see in the snow?**
   __ O __ __ __ __ __ __ __ __

7. **I can be opened and closed but do not have a handle?**
   __ O O __

8. **What eats grass while moooving across the fields?** __ O __

9. **I'm found in fossils but once walked the Earth.**
   __ __ __ __ O __ __ __ __ __

10. **I'm long and best when in a bun?** __ O __ __ O __

See page 127 for the answers.

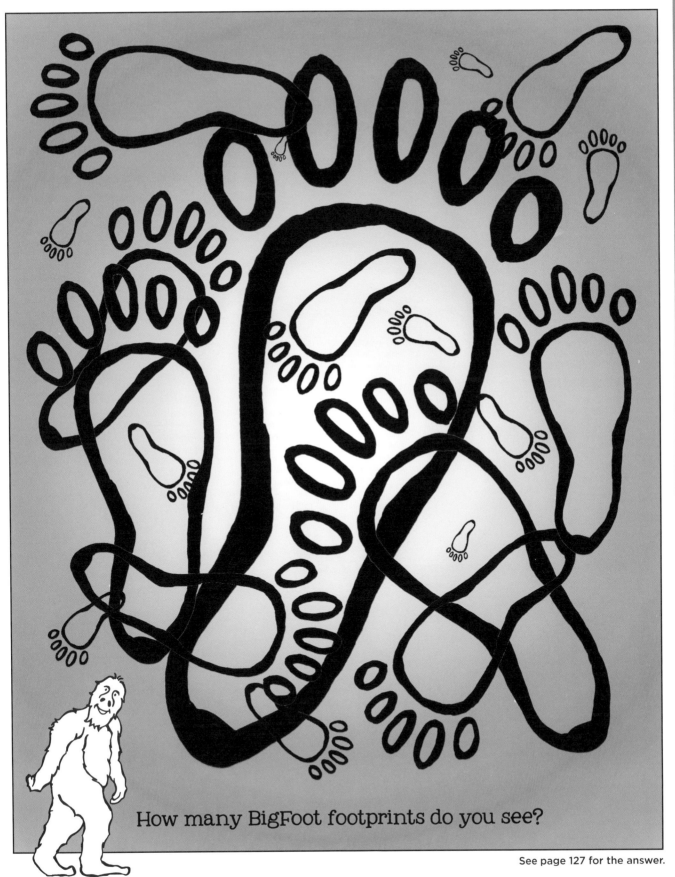

How many BigFoot footprints do you see?

See page 127 for the answer.

Cheetahs are the fastest animal in the world and can reach speeds up to 70 miles per hour (113 kph)!

Can you find 9 things different on this page?

Draw... Write... Imagine!

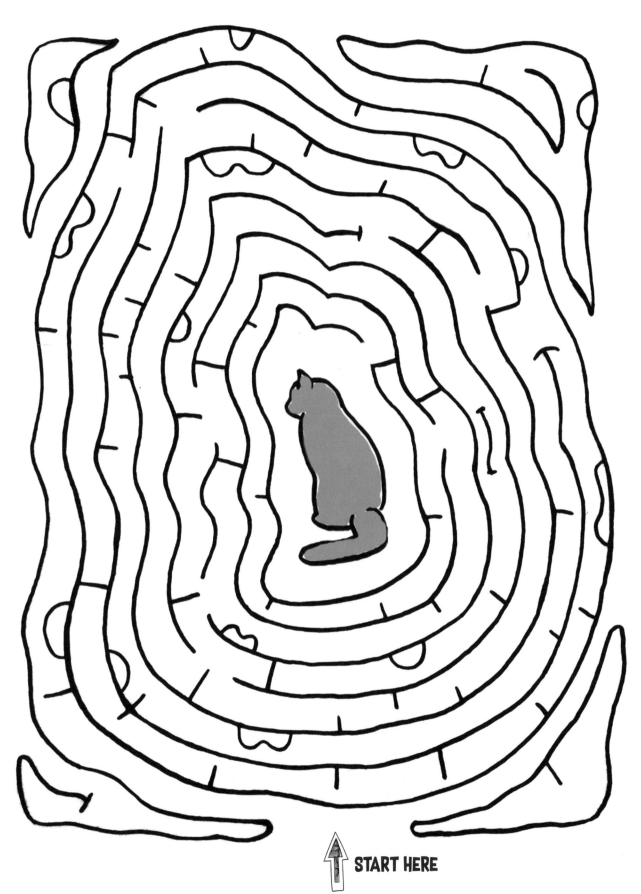

START HERE

Can you find the 10 giant pandas hiding
in this tower of giraffes?

Wild Animals

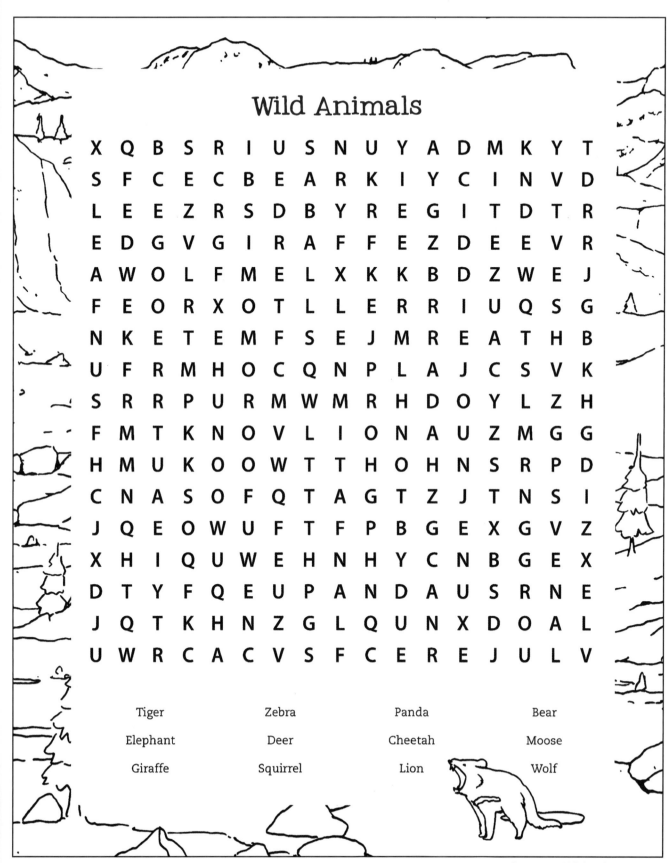

X Q B S R I U S N U Y A D M K Y T
S F C E C B E A R K I Y C I N V D
L E E Z R S D B Y R E G I T D T R
E D G V G I R A F F E Z D E E V R
A W O L F M E L X K K B D Z W E J
F E O R X O T L L E R R I U Q S G
N K E T E M F S E J M R E A T H B
U F R M H O C Q N P L A J C S V K
S R R P U R M W M R H D O Y L Z H
F M T K N O V L I O N A U Z M G G
H M U K O O W T T H O H N S R P D
C N A S O F Q T A G T Z J T N S I
J Q E O W U F T F P B G E X G V Z
X H I Q U W E H N H Y C N B G E X
D T Y F Q E U P A N D A U S R N E
J Q T K H N Z G L Q U N X D O A L
U W R C A C V S F C E R E J U L V

Tiger	Zebra	Panda	Bear
Elephant	Deer	Cheetah	Moose
Giraffe	Squirrel	Lion	Wolf

See page 128 for the answers.

Across

3 Moves up and down

4 Head of the class

6 Ribbit

8 Important to remember when jumping from a plane

10 2 wheels

Down

1 Holds us up

2 Where a river drops

5 Baseball has one

7 Has suction cups

9 Bends before the shoulder

See page 127 for the answers.

Can you solve these riddles?

Hint: All of the answers have the letter *R*.

1. **What is deeply rooted in the ground?**   __ r __ __ __

2. **What animal washes its hands and wears a mask?**
    R __ __ __ __ __ __ __

3. **What color always means STOP?**   R __ __ __

4. **Plants don't have a mouth but need this.**   __ __ __ __ __ r

5. **What has 4 wheels and a bed?**   __ r __ __ __ __

6. **A bee's favorite place to visit.**   __ __ __ __ __ __ r

7. **What is hard, sometimes smooth, sometimes very rough feeling?**   R __ __ __ __

8. **A nail needs this to move.**   __ __ __ __ __ __ r

9. **What moves slowly and carries its home?**   __ __ __ r __ __ __ __

10. **Who always has a long face?**   __ __ __ r __ __ __

See page 127 for the answers.

Can you finish drawing our knight on horseback?

Did you know a knight's suit of armor during medieval times could have weighed up to 110 pounds (50 kg)?

Did you know that birds came from a type
of dinosaur known as a theropod?

Can you find 9 things different on this page?

Can you find 8 things that don't fly?

Countries

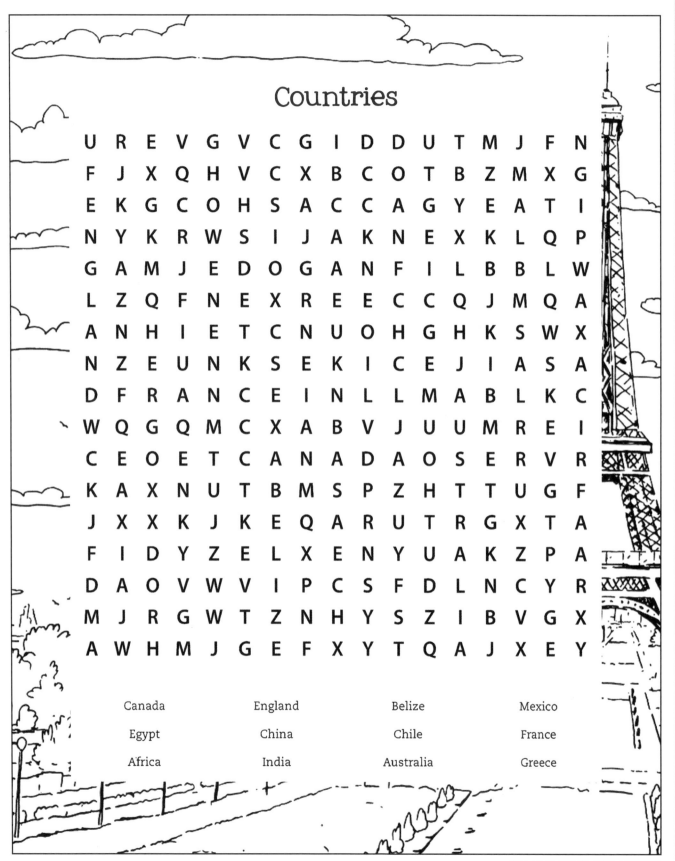

```
U R E V G V C G I D D U T M J F N
F J X Q H V C X B C O T B Z M X G
E K G C O H S A C C A G Y E A T I
N Y K R W S I J A K N E X K L Q P
G A M J E D O G A N F I L B B L W
L Z Q F N E X R E E C C Q J M Q A
A N H I E T C N U O H G H K S W X
N Z E U N K S E K I C E J I A S A
D F R A N C E I N L L M A B L K C
W Q G Q M C X A B V J U U M R E I
C E O E T C A N A D A O S E R V R
K A X N U T B M S P Z H T T U G F
J X X K J K E Q A R U T R G X T A
F I D Y Z E L X E N Y U A K Z P A
D A O V W V I P C S F D L N C Y R
M J R G W T Z N H Y S Z I B V G X
A W H M J G E F X Y T Q A J X E Y
```

Canada   England   Belize   Mexico

Egypt   China   Chile   France

Africa   India   Australia   Greece

See page 128 for the answers.

Can you finish drawing this scorpion?

Did you know there are over 2,000 kinds of scorpions around the world? And they love to live in hot, humid places.

Can you solve these riddles?

Hint: All of the answers have the letter *S.*

1. **I always look down but brighten your day!** S __ __

2. **What travels from dock to dock?** S __ __ __ __

3. **I'm very tiny but can build castles until a wave comes in to take me away!** S __ __ __ __

4. **What moves with the wind and rides the water?**
   S__ __ __ __ __ __ __ __

5. **People and horses hide behind my walls.** __ __ S __ __ __ __

6. **I have big antlers, live in the forest, and am a great swimmer.**
   __ __ __ S __ __

7. **What lives in the dirt and has a lot of blades?** __ __ __ __ S S

8. **What is right between your eyes but you can't see?** __ __ __ S __ __

9. **I'm a game played on a diamond.** __ __ __ S __ __ __ __ __

10. **I have a lot of teeth and can smell from a great distance.**
    S __ __ __ __ __

See page 127 for the answers.

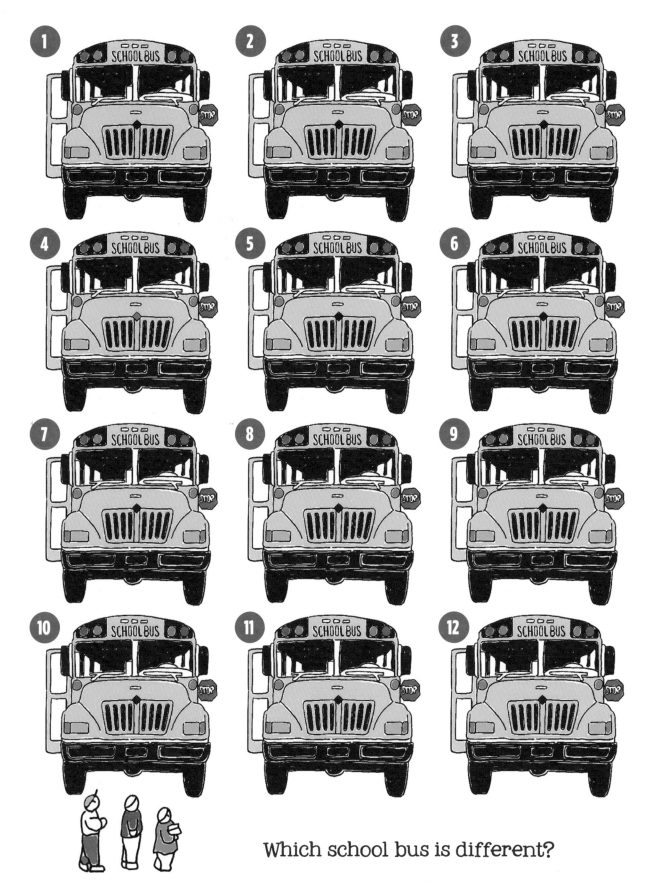

Which school bus is different?

See page 127 for the answer.

START HERE

Bears have 2 layers of fur: a short layer keeps
the bear warm and a long layer keeps water
away from the skin and short fur.

Draw... Write... Imagine!

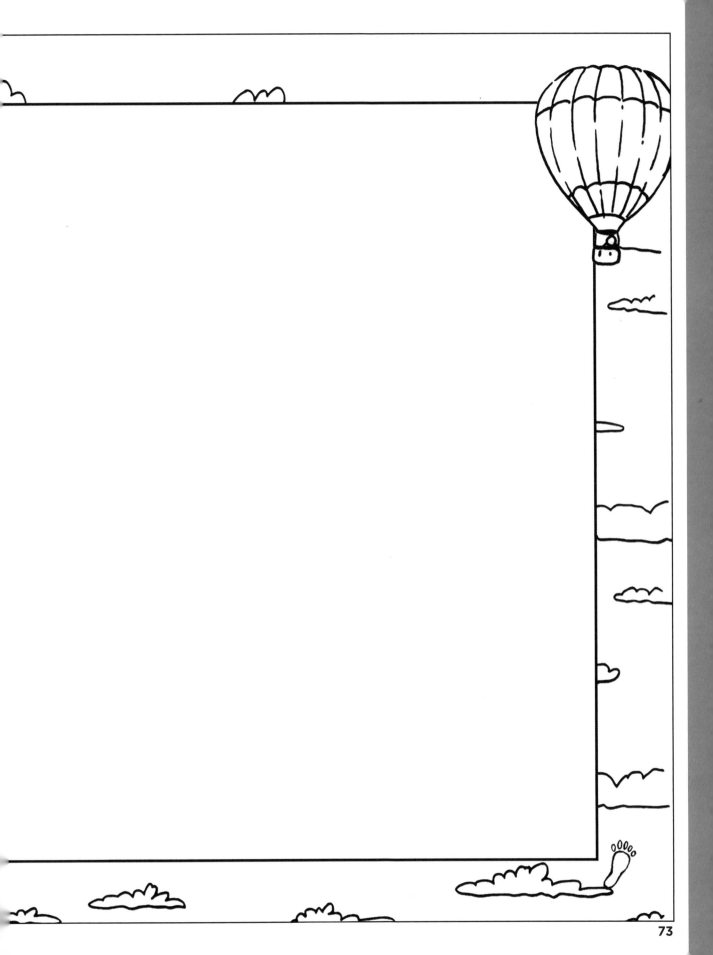

Insects

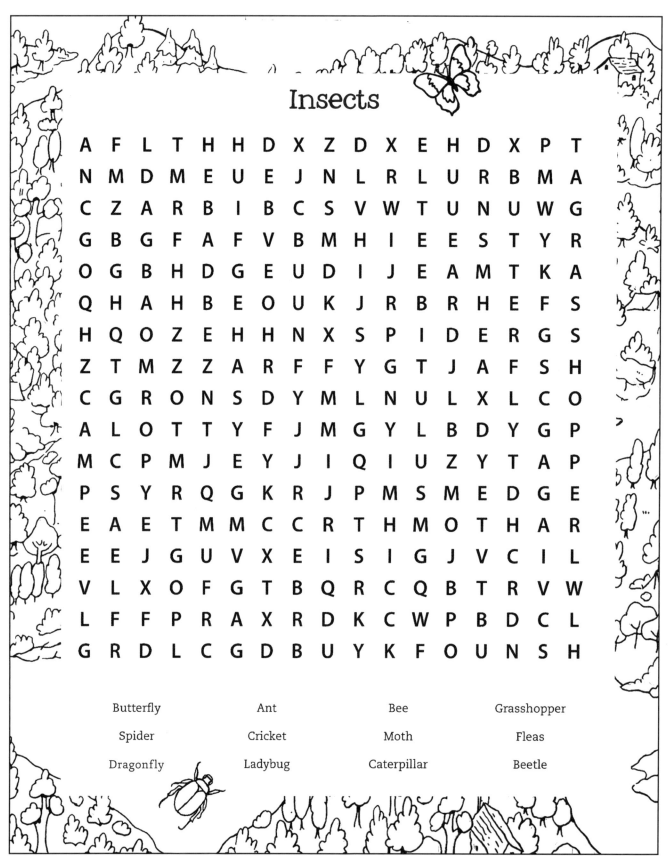

A F L T H H D X Z D X E H D X P T
N M D M E U E J N L R L U R B M A
C Z A R B I B C S V W T U N U W G
G B G F A F V B M H I E E S T Y R
O G B H D G E U D I J E A M T K A
Q H A H B E O U K J R B R H E F S
H Q O Z E H N X S P I D E R G S S
Z T M Z Z A R F F Y G T J A F S H
C G R O N S D Y M L N U L X L C O
A L O T T Y F J M G Y L B D Y G P
M C P M J E Y J I Q I U Z Y T A P
P S Y R Q G K R J P M S M E D G E
E A E T M M C C R T H M O T H A R
E E J G U V X E I S I G J V C I L
V L X O F G T B Q R C Q B T R V W
L F F P R A X R D K C W P B D C L
G R D L C G D B U Y K F O U N S H

Butterfly	Ant	Bee	Grasshopper
Spider	Cricket	Moth	Fleas
Dragonfly	Ladybug	Caterpillar	Beetle

See page 128 for the answers.

74

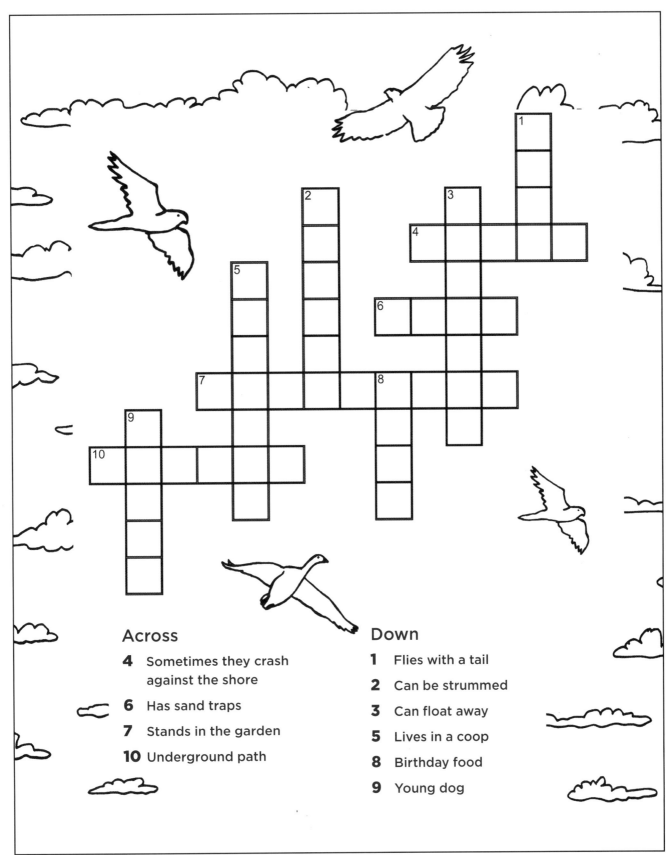

Across

4 Sometimes they crash against the shore

6 Has sand traps

7 Stands in the garden

10 Underground path

Down

1 Flies with a tail

2 Can be strummed

3 Can float away

5 Lives in a coop

8 Birthday food

9 Young dog

See page 127 for the answers.

Can you find and color every animal a different color?

Did you know a cow can eat up to 24 pounds (11 kg) of hay a day?

The Statue of Liberty took a team
of workers 9 years to build.

Can you find 9 things different on this page?

Can you solve these riddles?

Hint: All of the answers have the letter *T*.

1. **When stars come out.** __ __ __ __ __ t

2. **What is home to many but has no roof?** T__ __ __ __

3. **What BigFoot leaves behind but few have seen.**
__ __ __ __ t __ __ __ __ __ t

4. **I love the heat but am not a good hugger.** __ __ __ __ t __ __ __

5. **I once crawled on the ground as a caterpillar but can now see high above the trees.** __ __ t t __ __ __ __ __ __ __

6. **What can be used at home plate but is also known to fly at night?** __ __ __ t

7. **Sharks, sea turtles, and even tuna call me home.**
__ t __ __ __ __ t __ __ __ __ __ __ __ __ __

8. **Sometimes we have stripes, sometimes we don't. Sometimes we have long hair, sometimes we don't.** __ __ __ t __ __

9. **I hold a shirt together.** __ __ t t __ __ __

10. **What grows on a vine and loves the sun?** T__ __ __ __ t __

See page 127 for the answers.

Can you find the 10 bees and 10 beetles in this slew of bears?

Across

1 Duck, Goose

4 With meatballs

6 Giant river

8 26 of these

9 Rides a horse

Down

2 Needed in the winter

3 Opens a door

4 Found on the beach

5 Bald bird

7 Movie snack

See page 127 for the answers.

START HERE

A group of foxes is called a skulk or leash.

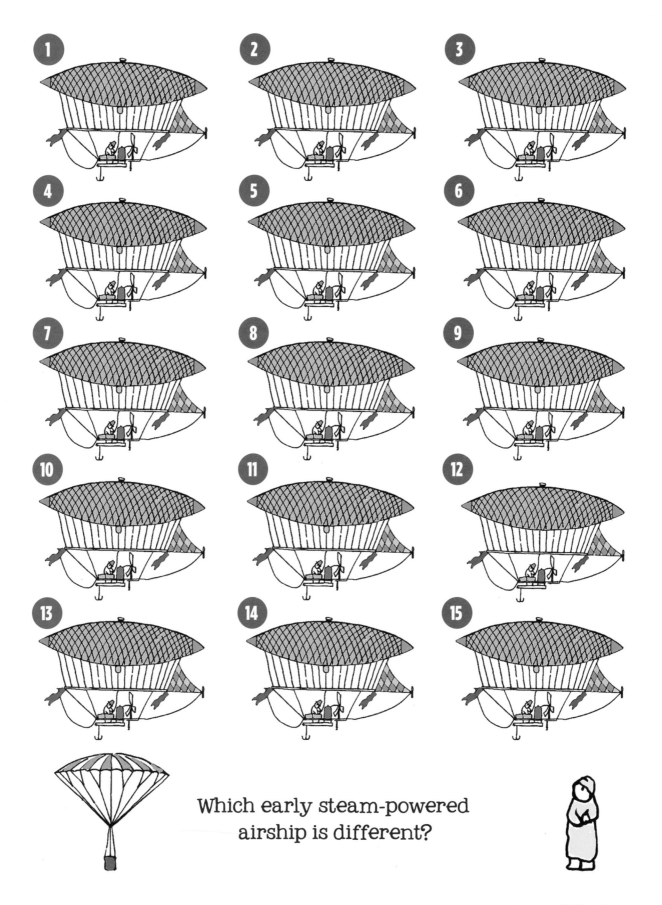

Which early steam-powered
airship is different?

See page 127 for the answer.

BigFoot's Famous Word Scramble

Hint: All the words on the list are types of **Colors.**

1. eprulp _ _ _ _ _ _

2. egenr _ _ _ _ _

3. akbcl _ _ _ _ _

4. onrbw _ _ _ _ _

5. itvloe _ _ _ _ _ _

6. ngroea _ _ _ _ _ _

7. ewthi _ _ _ _ _

8. lweyol _ _ _ _ _ _

9. ebul _ _ _ _

10. ayrg _ _ _ _

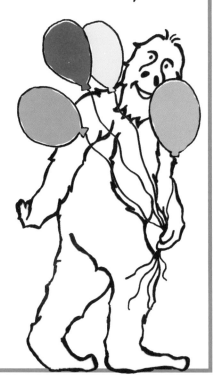

See page 127 for the answers.

85

Mammoths and other large, fur-covered animals lived during the last Ice Age, over 18,000 years ago.

Can you find **7 things** different on this page?

Fruits & Vegetables

```
R J I Q L N W Q I F K X J G K Z S
I N S J R A E P N E B B Z A E P R
F L Y T C E L E R Y E R N K N E M
A B U J B P I T V D E E P W C A K
T I I H I E K R N J T B I Z N S U
A S T P S G M H A L S M N O G L H
C H E R R I E S Y G B U E W Q E B
G F C B A N A N A F R C A Y P H C
K J I O M O N U X U L U P J M R W
Z M C A R R O T S U S C P M R Q I
M H S K J N D A K V E P L O Z G O
A X Q K X A E I P O Z U E J R B H
A U M X O J M O Q P G K G W D Y W
E I B V P D D V G H L W A C Y I E
A V E K M G W D X T X E Q G B D N
T E P X H H D W A T E R M E L O N
Z F Z L L R N P V E O R P I T M P
```

Carrots	Celery	Peas	Apple
Beets	Pineapple	Cherries	Pear
Corn	Banana	Cucumber	Watermelon

See page 128 for the answers.

Can you solve these riddles?

Hint: All of the answers have the letter *U*.

1. **What's hot but too far away to touch?** __ u __

2. **What changes night to day inside?** __ __ __ __ __ __ __ __ u __ __ __

3. **Jelly is my best friend!** __ __ __ __ __ u __ __ u __ __ __ __ __

4. **I have four partners on the right and left.** __ __ __ u __ __ __ __

5. **What can dive deep with many people?**
   __ u __ __ __ __ __ __ __ __

6. **Who can swim with the fish but has no gills?**
   __ __ __ u __ __ __ __ __ __ __ __

7. **I make great pies and can be carved.** __ u __ __ __ __ __ __ __

8. **People know this animal is near just by using their nose.**
   __ __ u __ __

9. **What can fly up, down, and even upside down?**
   __ u __ __ __ __ __ __ __ __ __ __

10. **When you're outside in the woods, you're in...**
    __ __ __ __ u __ __

See page 127 for the answers.

The first airship was built in 1852 by Henri Giffard and was powered by small steam engines.

Can you find 9 things that changed on this page?

Can you find 10 people with red umbrellas
among the red buses?

BigFoot's Famous Word Scramble

Hint: All the words on the list are types of **Dogs.**

1. icloel _ _ _ _ _ _

2. nstia dbreran

_ _ _ _ _ _ _ _ _ _ _ _

3. oelopd _ _ _ _ _ _

4. gnmrae dpserheh

_ _ _ _ _ _ _ _ _ _ _ _ _

5. neodlg eeirtervr

_ _ _ _ _ _ _ _ _ _ _ _ _ _

6. upg _ _ _

7. xbroe _ _ _ _ _

8. retreri _ _ _ _ _ _ _ _

9. lublgdo _ _ _ _ _ _ _

10. alebeg _ _ _ _ _ _

See page 127 for the answers.

Can you draw the other half of the beetle?

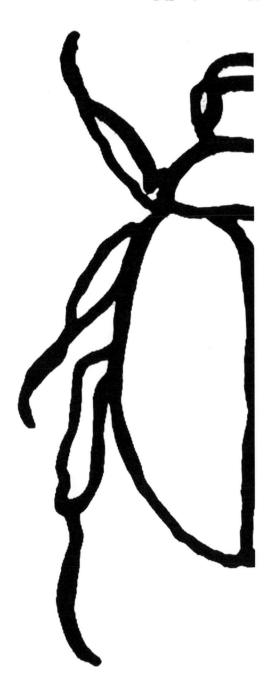

There are over 300,000 types of beetles around the world!

Across

1 Boat brake
5 Letter holder
6 Where plants start from
7 Found in a garden
10 Hops a lot

Down

2 Horse has four of them
3 A celebration
4 A car follows this
8 Cook with this
9 While you sleep

See page 127 for the answers.

The moon reflects light from the sun,
which is why it's so bright at nighttime.

Can you find **5 things** different on this page?

Can you find all 12 knights?

Can you solve these riddles?

Hint: All of the answers have the letter *W*.

1. **What is not a fish but has fins?** W_____

2. **Just when one ends, a new one starts.** W_____

3. **Favorite fruit for summertime.** W_____

4. **Banana's favorite color.** _____ W

5. **What lives in nature and is related to a dog?** W_____

6. **Put one foot in front of the other.** W_____

7. **I'm very fine!** ____ W_____

8. **Holes in trees are a hint they're near.** W_____

9. **What helps us move by going round and round?** W_____

10. **Where starfish live.** _____ W_____

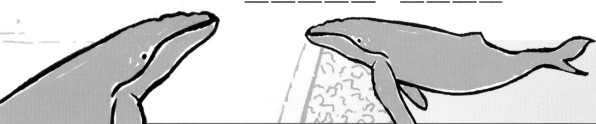

See page 127 for the answers.

Flowers can be found in every color of the rainbow. Color these flowers with your favorite colors!

How many different colors can you make your trees?

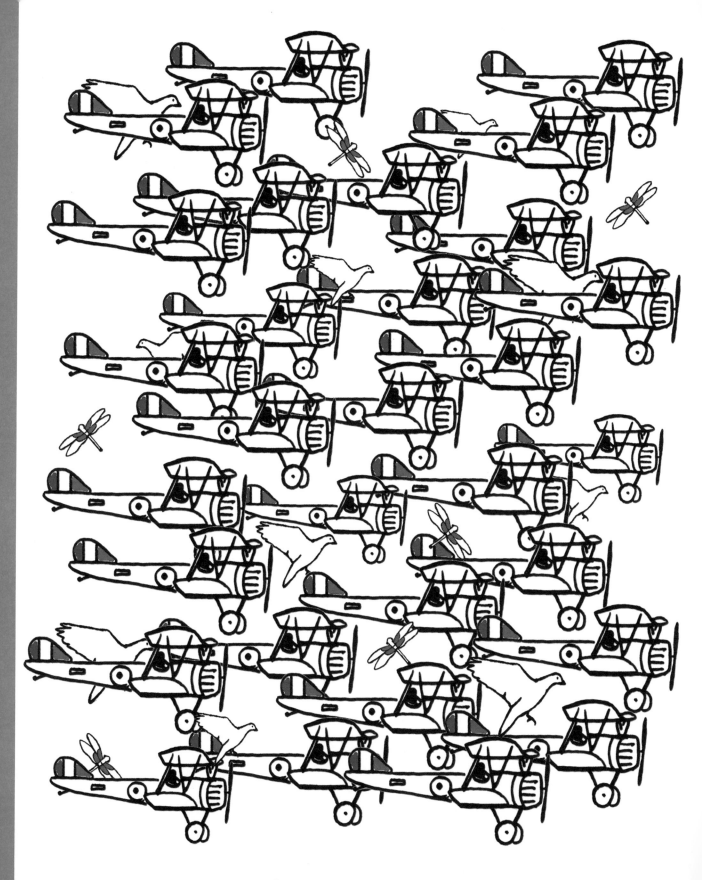

Can you find the **10 pigeons** flying with the planes?

Let's finish the sand castle!

Did you know the longest beach in the world is over 150 miles (241 m) long in Brazil? That's a lot of sand for sand castles!

Countries

```
K S J Q G U N I T E D S T A T E S
E B S R T O L G F X V L S S U C D
N K X D G I L A M C G L C O I X R
Y W X N L F I K Q W F I N P K A H
A V V G F I W D N A L A E Z W E N
K O P T O I T T O V X U G T O H D
J A A B L B W L L V Z Z T X I D E
R J L R M M Z B T S D A H C N G T
U D X A J J Q P A D C W L A P J K
V J U Z V B L S I H D O L S R A N
T V S I K N J T S H T E T Y R P Q
L N D L R R W I S Z R W U L Y A R
B C W T G D G T U I I Q G J A N R
S L O D U C F C R K Y Q Y K N N O
V Z X R S M O N G O L I A A N I D
I H C F I S P V S P A I N J M V Z
U E D J P F L G U V V O X A D F I
```

Chad	Ireland	Mongolia	Brazil
United States	Kenya	New Zealand	Spain
Japan	Mali	Scotland	Russia

See page 128 for the answers.

Let's finish drawing the giraffe!

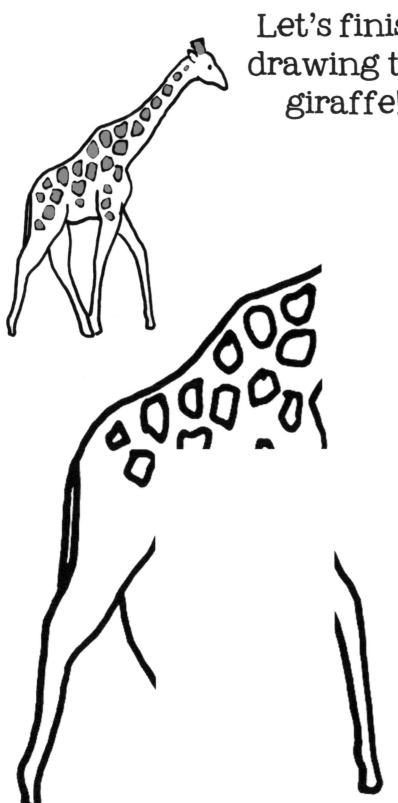

Did you know…

A giraffe's legs are taller than many humans at about 6 feet (1.8 m).

A giraffe can run as fast as 35 miles per hour (56 kph) over short distances.

A giraffe's neck is too short to reach the ground.

Orville and Wilbur Wright invented and flew the first powered airplane at Kitty Hawk, North Carolina, in 1903.

Can you find **8 things** different on this page?

Across

1 Long or short haired

4 Pink bird

6 Can be toasted over a fire

8 Large rock

9 Love picnics

Down

1 Funny person at the circus

2 Need syrup

3 Lava

5 Water all around

7 Always wears a suit

See page 127 for the answers.

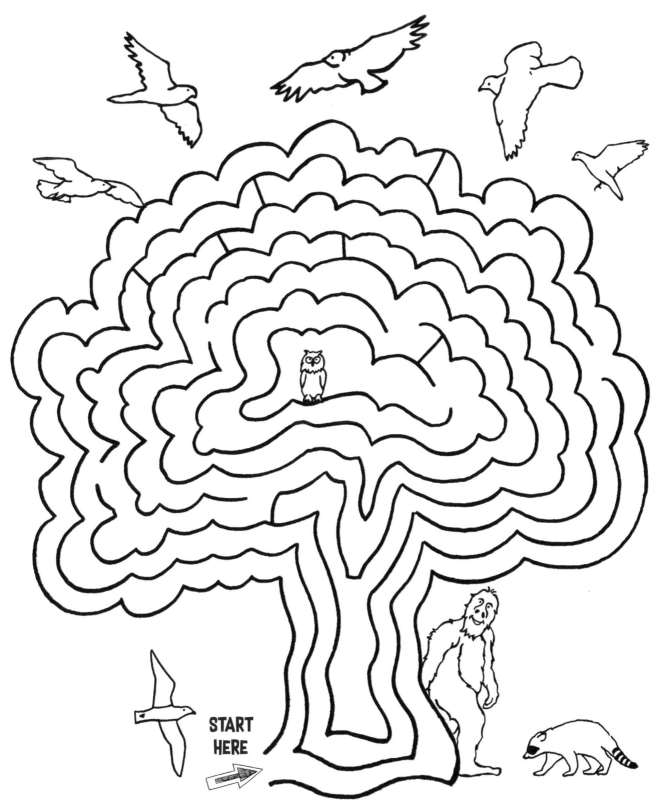

START HERE

How many different types of birds do you think live around the world?

Over 10,000... and we're still counting!

BigFoot's Famous Word Scramble

Hint: All the words on the list are types of **Wild Animals.**

1. etgir _ _ _ _ _

2. rbae _ _ _ _

3. penletha _ _ _ _ _ _ _ _

4. ezarb _ _ _ _ _

5. lwfo _ _ _ _

6. nloi _ _ _ _

7. meacl _ _ _ _ _

8. lraiolg _ _ _ _ _ _ _

9. ymknoe _ _ _ _ _ _

10. tshol _ _ _ _ _

See page 127 for the answers.

Can you finish drawing Saturn and the stars?

Did you know that Saturn is the second-largest planet in our solar system? Fabulous rings circle the planet. **Jupiter is the biggest planet!**

Draw... Write... Imagine!

Up, up, and away... it's time to color!

Plants

```
S L F T D I O S S X R I D B X Y L
D I S U N F L O W E R A G J A L M
N Y G P G Q V P V P M Y Z H U I T
N R E F B T D W R M R H I C J L U
F Y V V F P Z N C R N R L W H J F
A C G U I S M E B Y J X T M E S
O D M H N D S B V X B B A R P K M
R E A E R O E S H V H U Y Q L V Q
C U A I I L I A O N S O A O M O H
H M K F K X R L A M J Z O M G Y A
I I Q C I T C F E N F B R H G W V
D O U H O D A W F D M O A T D U G
S H B C L R C G D A N Y G M B P B
Y V I C N R T B B I F A M R I Q B
N D M N Z N U O H I Y U D L A Y U
R G K G B W S E I B V R U J V S Q
A X E N V H U F T A E T J Q C X S
```

Grass	Dandelion	Orchids	Ivy
Huckleberry	Fern	Lily	Cactus
Bamboo	Moss	Tulip	Sunflower

See page 128 for the answers.

Can you find 10 wombats walking with the woolly mammoths?

Let's finish drawing the dragon!

Stories from many, many years ago say that knights would fight fire-breathing dragons as a test of their bravery.

START
HERE

Did you know your foot has
26 bones, 33 joints, and 19 muscles?

120

BigFoot's Famous Word Scramble

Hint: All the words on the list are **States.**

1. iwhaia _ _ _ _ _ _

2. adoih _ _ _ _ _

3. emnia _ _ _ _ _

4. yadmnarl _ _ _ _ _ _ _ _

5. enw kryo _ _ _ _ _ _ _

6. dolfair _ _ _ _ _ _ _

7. sxate _ _ _ _ _

8. klsaaa _ _ _ _ _ _

9. anicafoirl _ _ _ _ _ _ _ _ _ _

10. wne cmxieo _ _ _ _ _ _ _ _ _

See page 127 for the answers.

Horse

Deer

Elephant

Cheetah

Kangaroo

Giraffe

Pigeon

Armadillo

1

2

3

4

5

6

7

8

Connect the footprint with the right animal.

See page 127 for the answers.

Can you find the 10 hummingbirds hiding in the hats?

The BIGFOOT™ FUN BOOK!

ANSWER KEY

Page 7: *Across*
2. River 5. Cabin 9. Mountain 10. Shark
Down
1. Lion 3. Rocket 4. BigFoot
6. Castle 7. Flower 8. Birds

Page 9: 1. Bear 2. Blanket 3. School bus 4. Bedtime
5. Baby 6. Umbrella 7. Zebra 8. Buffalo
9. Bumblebee 10. Beach ball

Page 12: 1. Eagle 2. Cardinal 3. Crow 4. Pigeon 5. Robin
6. Hawk 7. Ostrich 8. Buzzard 9. Dove
10. Bluebird

Page 19: 1. Desk 2. Apple 3. Bee 4. Snake 5. Ear
6. Elephant 7. House 8. Rose 9. Garden
10. Halloween

Page 22: *Across*
3. Umbrella 4. Apple 6. Monkey 8. Footprint
9. Donut
Down
1. Bus 2. Elephant 5. Clown 6. Money 7. Crow

Page 24: Trolley Car #9

Page 25: 1. Mountain 2. Island 3. Wrist 4. Lizard 5. Window
6. Tire 7. Bird 8. Train 9. Fish 10. Giraffe

Page 28: Dragon #6

Page 29: *Across*
3. Pencil 4. Dragon 6. Paintbrush 8. Football
9. Cardinal
Down
1. Barn 2. Piano 3. Parrot 5. Fire truck 7. Cookie

Page 33: Cardinal Fish #7

Page 39: *Across*
3. Spider 4. Minutes 5. Newspaper
7. Bridge 8. Horse 9. Museum
Down
1. Pyramids 2. Geese 6. Pretzel
7. Bread

Page 43: 1. Moon 2. Mountain
3. Camping 4. Hamburger
5. Map 6. Swamp 7. Mouse
8. Milk 9. Farm 10. Compass

Page 49: *Across*
1. Captain 3. Computer 5. Hamburger 6. Clouds
8. Candy 9. Oranges
Down
1. Checkers 2. Submarine 4. Cheetah
7. Nurse

Page 50: Viking Ship #3

Page 51: 1. Football 2. Checkers 3. Skiing 4. Bingo 5. Baseball 6. Chess 7. Tic-tac-toe 8. Tennis 9. Hockey 10. Soccer

Page 52: 1.BigFoot 2. Hoot 3. Octopus 4. Open 5. Ocean 6. Polar bear 7. Book 8. Cow 9. Dinosaur 10. Hot dog

Page 53: 20 footprints

Page 61: *Across*
3. Elevator 4. Teacher 6. Frog 8. Parachute 10. Bike
Down
1. Skeleton 2. Waterfall 5. Bat 7. Octopus 9. Elbow

Page 62: 1. Tree 2. Raccoon 3. Red 4. Water 5. Truck 6. Flower 7. Rock 8. Hammer 9. Turtle 10. Horse

Page 69: 1. Sun 2. Ship 3. Sand 4. Sailboat 5. Castle 6. Moose 7. Grass 8. Nose 9. Baseball 10. Shark

Page 70: School Bus #4

Page 75: *Across*
4. Waves 6. Golf 7. Scarecrow 10. Tunnel
Down
1. Kite 2. Guitar 3. Balloon 5. Chicken 8. Cake 9. Puppy

Page 80: 1. Night 2. Tree 3. Footprint 4. Cactus 5. Butterfly 6. Bat 7. Atlantic Ocean 8. Cats 9. Button 10. Tomato

Page 82: *Across*
1. Duck 4. Spaghetti 6. Mississippi 8. Letters 9. Cowboy
Down
2. Coat 3. Key 4. Seashells 5. Eagle 7. Popcorn

Page 84: Airship #12

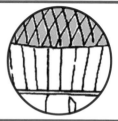

Page 85: 1. Purple 2. Green 3. Black 4. Brown 5. Violet 6. Orange 7. White 8. Yellow 9. Blue 10. Gray

Page 89: 1. Sun 2. Light bulb 3. Peanut butter 4. Thumbs 5. Submarine 6. Blue whale 7. Pumpkin 8. Skunk 9. Hummingbird 10. Nature

Page 93: 1. Collie 2. Saint Bernard 3. Poodle 4. German shepherd 5. Golden retriever 6. Pug 7. Boxer 8. Terrier 9. Bulldog 10. Beagle

Page 97: *Across*
1. Anchor 5. Envelope 6. Seeds 7. Vegetables 10. Rabbit
Down
2. Hooves 3. Festival 4. Road 8. Skillet 9. Dream

Page 101: 1. Whale 2. Week 3. Watermelon 4. Yellow 5. Wolf 6. Walk 7. Powder 8. Woodpecker 9. Wheel 10. Underwater

Page 110: *Across*
1. Cat 4. Flamingo 6. Marshmallow 8. Boulder 9. Ants
Down
1. Clown 2. Pancakes 3. Volcano 5. Island 7. Penguin

Page 112: 1. Tiger 2. Bear 3. Elephant 4. Zebra 5. Wolf 6. Lion 7. Camel 8. Gorilla 9. Monkey 10. Sloth

Page 121: 1. Hawaii 2. Idaho 3. Maine 4. Maryland 5. New York 6. Florida 7. Texas 8. Alaska 9. California 10. New Mexico

Page 122: 1. Giraffe 2. Armadillo 3. Pigeon 4. Kangaroo 5. Horse 6. Deer 7. Elephant 8. Cheetah

WORD SEARCH KEY

Page 17:

Oceans & Seas

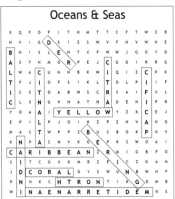

Page 26:

Birds

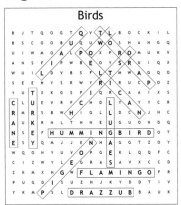

Page 32:

Farm Animals

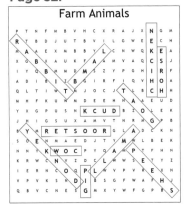

Page 46:

Trees

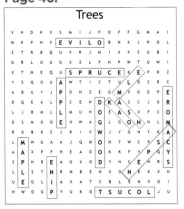

Page 60:

Wild Animals

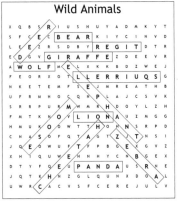

Page 67:

Countries

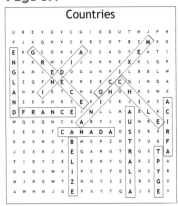

Page 74:

Insects

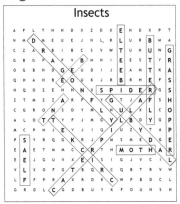

Page 88:

Fruits & Vegetables

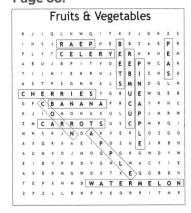

Page 106:

Countries

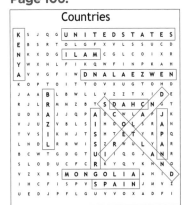

Page 117:

Plants

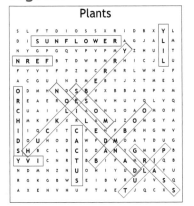

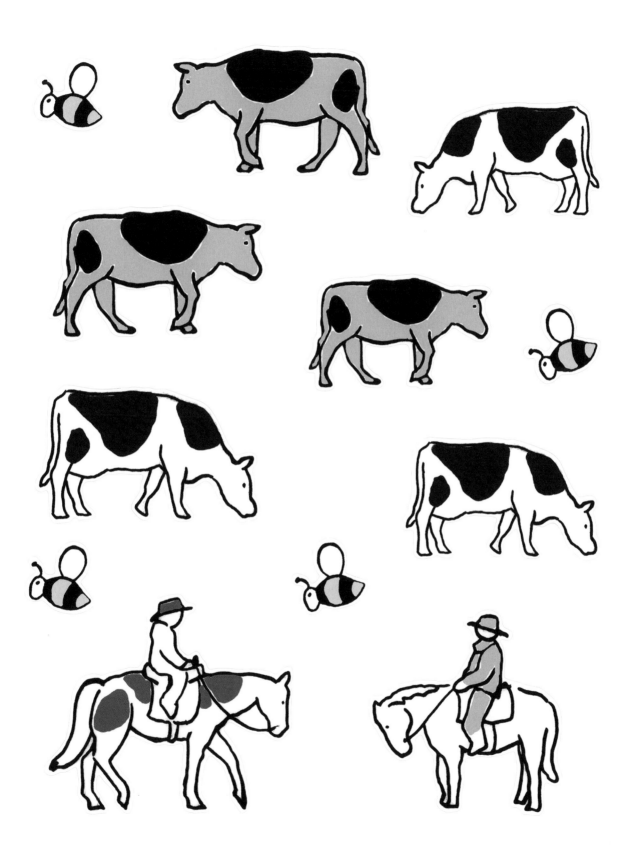

135

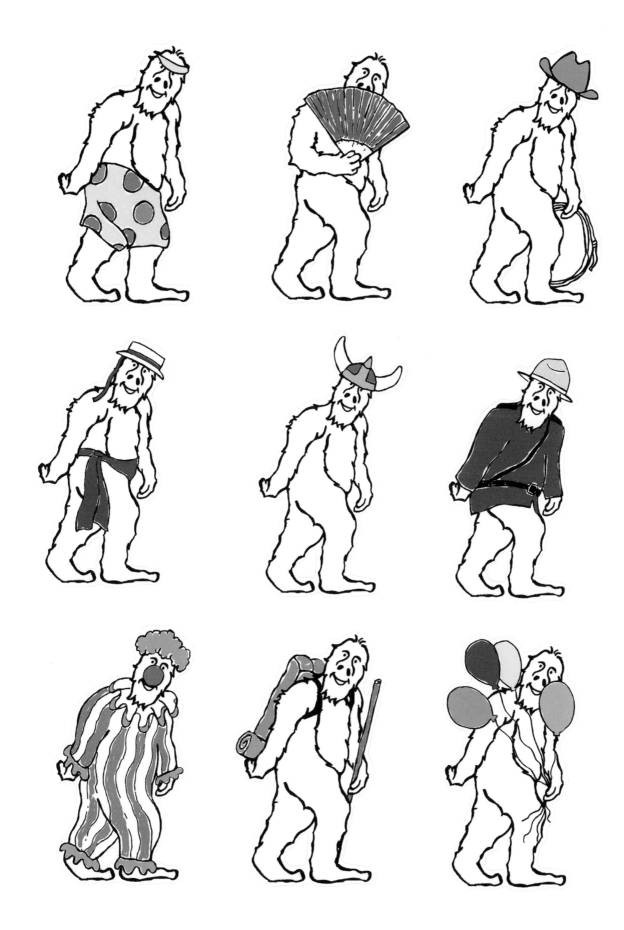